MY HAMSTER IS A
PIRATE

MY HAMSTER IS A PIRATE

DAVE LOWE

ILLUSTRATED BY THE BOY FITZ HAMMOND

Piccadilly
PRESS

First published in Great Britain in 2012 by
PICCADILLY PRESS

This edition published in 2019 by
PICCADILLY PRESS
80–81 Wimpole St, London W1G 9RE
www.piccadillypress.co.uk

A CIP catalogue record for this book is available
from the British Library.

ISBN: 978-1-84812-785-2
Also available as an ebook

1

Printed and bound in Great Britain by Clays Ltd, Elcograf S.p.A.

Piccadilly Press is an imprint of Bonnier Books UK
www.bonnierbooks.uk

*To my nephew and niece James and Edith –
ahoy there, me hearties!*

And with thanks to Miri and Rebecca for all the ideas.

THE JINKS FAMILY
Me, Lucy, Mum Dad and Stinky

Chapter 1

We were having egg and chips when my dad coughed. At first I thought he might have got a chip stuck in his throat. But no – he was coughing to get our attention.

'Your mum and I have got some great news,' he said.

'Are we finally getting a pony?' squealed Lucy, my little sister.

'A baby brother?' I asked.

'No and no,' Mum said, very quickly. 'Absolutely not.'

Dad said the next bit really slowly, leaving a big gap between each word to get us even more excited: 'We. Are. Going. To . . .'

'The ballet?' gasped Lucy.

'The moon?' I said.

'The beach!' Dad announced. 'For a holiday. Tomorrow!'

He grinned and waited for us to whoop with joy.

We didn't.

'But I'll miss my dance class,' Lucy moaned.

She tap-danced a lot. A tap-tap-tapping sound came from her bedroom pretty much all the time. Living with Lucy was like living with a moody woodpecker.

'It's only for one week,' my dad explained.

'And what about Delilah?' Lucy asked. Delilah was her cat. 'What will we do with her?'

'She'll be fine,' my mum said. 'We're taking her to a cattery.'

'What's a cattery?' asked Lucy.

'It's a place where they look after your cat while you're away. It's like a hotel for cats.'

Lucy's eyes lit up.

'That sounds great,' she said. 'Can I stay there, instead of going on holiday with you?'

'It's for cats only,' said Dad, frowning. 'Not for cats and people.' He shook his head. 'You know, most normal kids are actually excited about going on holiday. What about you, Ben? You're hardly jumping for joy either.'

'I am,' I said. 'Inside. It's just – what will we do about Stinky?'

Stinky was my pet hamster, and I was the only one who knew that he was a genius – a genius who got really bored when he was alone, even for one day.

'I didn't even think about Stinky,' Dad admitted. 'Can't we just put a whole carrot in his cage and leave him here?'

I shook my head and, luckily, Mum shook her head too.

'And I guess we can't ask the neighbours to look after him,' Dad added. He was right about that. We had the worst next-door neighbours in the world.

'Is there such a thing as a hamsterery?' Lucy asked.

'A what?' said Dad.

'A hamsterery. Like a cattery, but for hamsters.'

My dad shook his head and chuckled.

'It's a very good idea though – a holiday home for rodents. We could open a business and call it the Hamster Hotel. The Mouse House! The Guinea Pigsty! The Rattery!'

'You're not helping, Derek,' my mum said.

'Can we take Stinky with us, Mum?' I said. 'Dad? Please? He'll be no trouble.'

My parents looked at each other. Dad shrugged.

'I suppose we'll have to,' Mum said.

'Woo-hoo!' I said, and straight after tea I rushed to tell Stinky the good news.

He didn't look nearly as excited as I'd hoped though. In fact he looked a bit grumpy.

'Come on, Stinky! A beach holiday! It'll be awesome! The sun on your fur! The sand between your tiny toes!'

'But I won't *be* on the beach,' he snapped. 'I'll be stuck indoors in this cage. And in any case, why would I want to go to the beach?

There will be seagulls and crabs – neither of which will ever have seen a hamster before. They won't take long, however, to work out that I look like a very tasty meal indeed.'

'But you were saying only yesterday how boring your life is, Stinky. A holiday might be full of adventure.'

'Adventure?' he said with a sigh. 'Like what, for example?'

'We could search for buried treasure. I'll take my bucket and spade, just in case.'

He groaned.

'You've been watching too many movies, Ben. I expect that you think we'll discover a treasure map and "X" will mark the spot.'

I shrugged. 'You never know,' I said.

Chapter 2

Every time we arrive on holiday, the first thing that my mum does is have a cup of tea. The first thing that my dad does (after making my mum a cup of tea) is go out and get a local newspaper. 'To get a flavour of the place,' he says. 'To see what's going on.'

The first thing that Lucy and I do, however, is burst through the door of wherever we're staying and race each other to get the best bedroom. I'm nine and she's seven, so I always win.

Not this time though.

This time Lucy ran in ahead of me, because I was carrying the cage with Stinky inside, and if I dropped him, he would never let me forget it.

After I put the cage onto the bedside table of the smaller bedroom, I sat on the bed and waited for him to come out of his little house.

'Hey, Stinky,' I said. 'We're here.'

When he finally poked his head out, he sniffed a lot and scrunched up his face. The sheet of newspaper that lined his cage was dotted with lots of little hamster poos.

'My cage needs cleaning out,' he said.

'I did it only yesterday,' I reminded him.

'I poo more when I'm nervous,' he

explained. 'And, with your dad driving, there is a great deal to be nervous about. Unlike you, I wasn't wearing a seatbelt. And another thing –'

Stinky suddenly stopped talking because

my dad himself came into the room, waving the local newspaper and grinning.

'Look what I've seen,' said Dad, thrusting the paper into my hands.

I groaned.

Mum was brilliant at making costumes, Dad loved competitions and Lucy adored dressing up. This was a terrible combination, as far as I

FANCY-DRESS FAMILY DISCO

PRIZE FOR
THE BEST-DRESSED FAMILY

was concerned. Last year, for a birthday party, we'd gone as Goldilocks and the Three Bears. I was Baby Bear, in a bear outfit with a nappy on. It was all very, very embarrassing.

'Come on, Ben,' Dad said, ruffling my hair. 'It'll be fun! And, speaking of fun, let's go to the beach! You've never really arrived at the seaside until you've dipped your toes into freezing cold water.'

I got changed into my shorts and, before I left, I cleaned out the cage and used a fresh piece of Dad's newspaper to line it. This cheered Stinky up – a little bit at least.

When we came back from the beach, three hours later, he was like a different hamster. He was pacing excitedly in his cage and, when I held out a couple of shells for him to inspect, he wasn't at all interested.

'Never mind shells, Ben,' he said. 'I have a feeling that there might be some actual treasure around here. *Buried* treasure.'

I stared back at him in disbelief.

'Didn't someone tell me that people only found buried treasure in movies?'

'Well, that's what I thought. While you were playing in the sand, however, I did a little reading.'

He tapped a paw onto the piece of newspaper that was under his feet, and I read the headline through the bars of his cage.

'There once was a man,' Stinky began, 'by the name of Algernon Pickles, who lived very

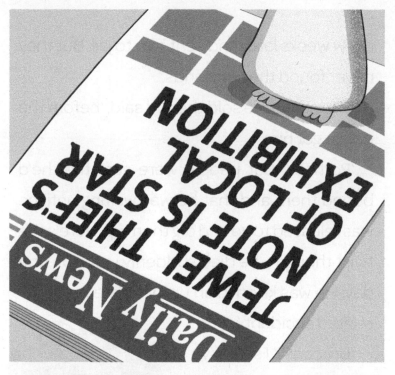

close to here, and who, twenty years ago, robbed a jeweller's in this very town. He stole eight pink diamonds, each of them only as big as the nail on your little finger, but worth a great deal of money. The police caught him a few weeks later and sent him to jail. But they never found the diamonds.'

'He must have sold them,' I said, 'before the police got him.'

'Perhaps. But people were sure that he'd buried them and that he was waiting until he was released to go and dig them up. Here's the twist though – he died suddenly in prison one day. He was killed in an unfortunate broccoli-related accident.'

'Broccoli?' I said. 'I've always told Mum it could kill me! I was right!'

'Anyway,' Stinky continued, ignoring me, 'when they were cleaning out his prison cell, they found a single piece of paper in his drawer.'

'A treasure map!' I said. 'I knew it!'

Stinky rolled his eyes.

'Of course it wasn't a treasure map. If it had been a treasure map, don't you think that someone would have read it and discovered the treasure by now?'

'I suppose so.'

'On that small piece of paper were these words, in Algernon Pickles's handwriting: "Crime never pays". And that may well be true. But that is not what interests me. What interests me is what was on the other side of the note. Something rather odd.'

'Odd?'

'A shopping list.'

I frowned.

'What's so strange about a shopping list? My mum and dad make them all the time.'

'Do you think there are any shops in prison?' Stinky asked. I shrugged. 'Of course there aren't,' he said impatiently. 'Being in prison isn't like being on holiday, you know. Prisons are not nice places at all.'

'Well, I know *that*. Apparently they even make you eat broccoli.'

'So,' said Stinky, 'if there are no shops in jail, why on earth would Algernon Pickles have a shopping list?'

'Maybe he was writing down all the things he'd buy as soon as he got out.'

'Perhaps. But the newspaper doesn't mention what was on the list. And furthermore, he wasn't due to be released for a very long time. This is what I think: that the shopping list might be a code – a code which tells us where to find the diamonds. And you, Benjamin Jinks, need to go to the museum to find out.'

Chapter 3

While we were all having breakfast the next morning, Dad asked us what we'd like to do for the day.

Mum said she was going to do a bit of work on the pirate costumes she was making for the fancy-dress disco, and then spend the rest of the day lying on the beach, reading a book and stuffing her face with chocolate ice cream.

Lucy said she'd like to practise some new dance steps after breakfast, before cooling down with a swim in the sea.

'And you, Ben?' asked Dad.

I said: 'I want to go to the museum.'

Everyone stared at me. My dad paused his spoonful of cornflakes just before it got to his mouth.

'The where?' he asked, frowning, as if he'd misheard.

'The museum.'

Lucy giggled.

'There's an exhibition on, about local crime,' I said.

My dad shook his head in disbelief.

'We're on *holiday*, Ben,' he said. 'An actual *beach* is just out there. The sea is blue. The sun's shining. And you want to go to a museum?'

'Yes, please.'

He sighed.

'Maybe tomorrow,' he said. 'If it rains.'

Mum put down her cup of tea and frowned at Dad.

'We should be encouraging Ben,' she told him. 'He hardly ever wants to do anything educational.'

'The *beach* is educational,' said my dad. 'All those pebbles. Shells. Crabs. It's nature, right on our very doorstep.

But then Mum gave Dad one of her special looks, and we all knew he'd be taking me.

In fact, my dad took me to the museum straight after breakfast.

It was a small building, and the sign on the

door said that entry was free, which made my
dad a tiny bit happier. He was a very big fan of
free stuff.

When we walked in, the grey-haired man who worked there – who'd been dozing in a chair – woke up with a start.

He was tall, wearing a name badge, and looked very surprised to see us.

Ted Slim rubbed his eyes and cleared his throat. 'Welcome,' he said, in the whispery voice of people who spend a lot of time in libraries and museums. 'We don't get many visitors on beautiful days like today. Most people are out relaxing on the beach.'

'Of course they are,' my dad said, looking at me and shaking his head. 'Why wouldn't they be?'

'We came to see the crime exhibition, please,' I said.

The museum only had one room, and Ted Slim pointed us in its direction.

'If you have any questions,' he said, 'I'll be right here.'

And then he closed his eyes and went back to sleep.

The first exhibit was an old fake banknote in a glass display case. Next was a newspaper report from a kidnapping one hundred years ago. After that was a 'Wanted' posted.

But it was the next exhibit that I'd come to see – the Mystery of the Missing Diamonds.

In a glass display case was the newspaper article from the day after the robbery. Next to that was the front page of the newspaper from a few weeks later. Then came a photo of

Algernon Pickles himself and, finally, the note.

When my dad wandered off to look at something else, I tried to slide open the glass top of the cabinet, so I could flip the note and read what was on the back. But it was locked and there was no way to open it. I walked around the case, disappointed, looking for another way in.

There was a small round hole, in the back of the case, just big enough to fit a ping-pong ball, but much too small for my hand.

My dad was getting fidgety. We left soon after.

I hadn't given up hope of reading the shopping list, though. Because I had a plan.

The hole in the back of the case might have been too small for a hand. But it was just big enough for a hamster.

Chapter 4

'Absolutely not,' Stinky said, as soon as I got back to our room and told him about my incredible plan.

'Oh, come on,' I said. 'You're clever, and clever people *love* museums.'

'That may be correct,' he sniffed, 'but I'm not a person, in case you hadn't noticed. I'm a hamster. And clever hamsters keep well clear of museums. Because, Ben, the only animals you will ever see in museums are ones that are stuffed. And I,' he added, 'most certainly do not want to be stuffed.'

'I thought you might be excited. It's an adventure! And in the newspaper it said that the diamonds are all five carat. You love carrots, Stinky.'

He rolled his eyes.

'If you could spell properly,' he said, 'you'd know that it's an entirely different word. "Carat" – C–A–R–A–T – means how big they are. A five-carat diamond, for example, is –'

'As big as five carrots?'

He sighed. 'If I agree to go with you,' he said irritably, 'will you stop annoying me right now, and leave me alone so I can have a nap? And get me five *actual* carrots?'

'Sure!' I said. 'So you'll do it?'

He nodded reluctantly.

'But first,' I said, 'I've got to get Dad to take me to the museum again, and he didn't even want to go the first time.'

'I can't believe I'm going to do this, but – go

now and ask your dad if he'll take you back there tomorrow if it rains.'

I did. Dad took one look out of the window at the clear blue sky, grinned and said, 'Sure.'

Then I went back to Stinky.

'Now what do I need to do?' I asked him.

'Nothing. It's going to rain tomorrow.'

'How do you know?'

'It's instinctive, Ben. Animals are far more sensitive to changes in the weather than humans. Birds, for example, know that wet weather is coming a long time before people do. Dogs start barking well before a storm. And as for hamsters, we get this tingling sensation in our fur when rain is on the way.'

'Wow,' I said. 'Really?'

'No,' he said, poking a paw at the sheet of newspaper lining his cage, 'I just read tomorrow's weather forecast in the paper, right here.'

Chapter 5

Stinky was right. It was pouring the next morning, and Dad and me were dripping wet as we walked into the museum.

'You again?' Ted Slim whispered, rubbing his eyes. He'd been dozing in his chair again. 'You're my best customers, you two.'

'He's doing some kind of project,' my dad said, pointing out the pen and the little pad of paper I was holding.

'Well, I'm here if you need me,' Ted Slim said with a yawn. 'I'm just going to study the backs of my eyelids for a moment.'

Then he rested his head on his hand and closed his eyes.

'Now, that's a job I'd like to have,' Dad whispered to me. 'Never a moment's excitement. Lots of time to have a nap or do the crossword. Speaking of which, I'll just be over here with the newspaper.'

As my dad sat down and started on the crossword, I went straight to the note, hoping to solve my own puzzle.

Stinky was wriggling nervously in my pocket.

When we got to the back of the display case, I took him out and put him onto the palm of my hand.

But, now that he was here, I realised that

the hole was
pretty small, even
for him. I sighed.
  'Sorry, Stinky,' I
whispered sadly.
'There's no way
you'll squeeze –'

I hadn't even finished my sentence when Stinky thrust forward, wriggled and writhed and somehow managed to push his way into the hole. I'd forgotten just how good hamsters are at burrowing.

When he was halfway in, though, disaster struck – he got stuck. His bottom was still wiggling crazily, but he wasn't budging at all.

In a panic, I glanced at my dad. His head

was still behind the newspaper. Ted Slim was still asleep. But Stinky was still stuck, no matter how much he struggled and squirmed. Not knowing what else to do, I gave his bottom a gentle push. Nothing happened. So I pushed it a bit harder, and this time it worked.

Stinky tumbled clumsily inside the case and – when he got to his feet – scampered over to the note, nudged his nose underneath and managed to flip it over.

And there it was, in Algernon Pickles's own

handwriting: the shopping list.

We both stared at it.

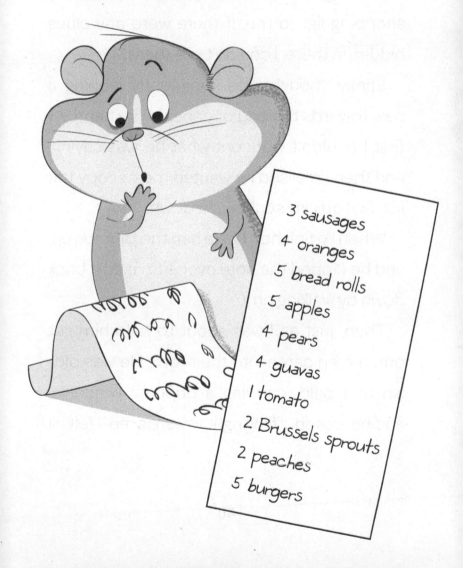

3 sausages
4 oranges
5 bread rolls
5 apples
4 pears
4 guavas
1 tomato
2 Brussels sprouts
2 peaches
5 burgers

I sighed. I don't know what I'd been expecting, but this looked just like an ordinary shopping list to me. If there were any clues hidden in there, I couldn't see them.

Stinky, though, was impatiently jabbing a paw towards the pad of paper in my hand. At first I couldn't work out what he was saying, and then I realised he wanted me to copy the list. So I quickly scribbled it down.

When I'd finished I gave him the thumbs up, and he flipped the note over and fixed it back down by walking on it.

Then, just as I was about to help him get out, a man came into the room. He was old-ish and bald, carrying a dripping umbrella, and he was shuffling right towards me. I felt all panicky. What would happen if he discovered a hamster in the display case?

I mouthed the word 'hide' to Stinky. He glanced around nervously, searching for a hiding place. Then he scurried off to the newspaper front page, which was next to the note, and managed to wriggle underneath it, like it was a bedsheet.

He was only just in time, because the man stopped right next to me and peered into the case. Like many bald men, he had plenty of hair in other places to make up for having none on top of his head. His eyebrows were bushy. Tufts of hair sprouted from his ears. Chest hair poked out of his shirt collar.

I waited for him to move on to look at the other exhibits so that Stinky could come out, but the man was just staring at the note. Nothing else seemed to interest him at all. This was good in a way, because it meant that he hadn't noticed the hamster-shaped lump under the newspaper page right beside it. But he kept on looking at the note and didn't move at all. Finally he turned to me.

'There's lots of other things to see, you know, kid,' he said irritably, gesturing to the rest of the museum.

I nodded nervously. I wanted to move, I really did – there was something frightening about the man – but I couldn't leave Stinky, even for a minute.

The man cracked his knuckles one by one and hissed menacingly, 'Beat it!'

I gulped and my legs went all wobbly. I looked at my dad – he glanced up but then went straight back to his crossword. As for Ted Slim, he was actually snoring now. But the bald man was still glaring at me.

'Scram,' he snarled.

I edged away and pretended to look at another exhibit, making sure I could still see his reflection in the glass.

He checked that no one was looking, and then took a paperclip out of his trouser pocket, stretched it out so it was like a piece of wire and – in one smooth movement – wiggled it into the lock on top of the glass case, twisted it and then slid the glass open. Next, he lifted out the note, folded it, stuffed it into his pocket, slid the glass top shut and strolled out of the museum, twirling his umbrella.

Chapter 6

I wanted to yell, 'Stop! Thief!' like they do in the movies, so that my dad would spring into action, but first I had to rescue Stinky.

The glass top of the display case was shut, but now unlocked. I edged over to it and whispered, 'Stinky! Come out – quick!'

He shrugged off the newspaper. I checked that no one was watching, slid it open, glanced around again – and reached in. Stinky scurried over to my hand. I lifted him out and, as soon as he was safely in my pocket, I yelled, 'Dad!'

That man just stole something!

My dad's head suddenly appeared from behind his newspaper and Ted Slim woke up with a start.

'That man just stole something!' I shouted.

'Which man?' Ted Slim said, leaping up from his chair and looking around. He rushed over to me, skidded to a stop and stared at the place where the note used to be. His voice was now nothing at all like a whisper. 'My good goodness!' he exclaimed. 'The centrepiece of our exhibition! It's been pinched!'

Dad, meanwhile, had darted outside, but soon came back shaking his head.

'No sign of him,' he announced. 'On the plus side, the rain has stopped.'

Ted Slim, looking suddenly pale, picked up the phone, called the police, and we all stood there, waiting for them to arrive.

'Did you get a good look at him?' Ted Slim asked.

Dad shook his head. 'He was bald, that's all I noticed. An older bald bloke. Had an umbrella.'

'I didn't get a really good look at him either,' Ted Slim admitted.

This was hardly surprising.

Then they both turned to me.

'He had mean eyes,' I said. 'Bushy eyebrows. Hairy ears.'

'Maybe you should draw a picture,' Dad suggested. 'For the police.' He nodded at the notebook I was clutching.

'You know how rubbish I am at drawing, Dad,' I protested.

'Being bad at something never stopped a Jinks,' he said proudly. 'We always give everything a try, no matter how completely useless we are.'

'Take a seat,' said Ted Slim, eagerly offering me his chair and desk.

I sat down – very, very carefully, so I didn't squash Stinky. And I started to draw.

When I had finished, I tore the page out of the notebook and showed it to them.

'So,' Ted Slim said, unimpressed, 'we're looking for a man with a head shaped like a football, with one eye bigger than the other and whose ears are in the wrong place?'

'Good try, son,' Dad said, ruffling my hair. 'Picasso wasn't any good at drawing faces either. And his pictures sell for millions.'

My picture must actually have been OK though, because when the police officer came, she listened to my story and took one look at the drawing before saying, 'Oh yes! It's Larry "The Key" Skinner! I'd know that face anywhere. He's a burglar whose speciality is unpicking locks. No door – or museum display case, it would seem – is safe from Larry Skinner. But I thought he'd retired. Stealing an old note with "Crime never pays" on it seems very . . . What's the word?'

'Ironic,' said Stinky, unable to stop himself. His voice was muffled by my pocket and luckily everyone thought it was me talking.

'Ironic, yes,' said the police officer.

Dad stared at me, his expression a mixture of stunned and impressed.

'*Ironic,*' he repeated. 'That's a fancy word, for you, Ben. Nice work.'

The police officer went away to talk into her walkie-talkie, and when she came back she looked even more puzzled.

'It turns out that Larry Skinner was an associate of Algernon Pickles – the diamond thief himself.'

Stinky wriggled in my pocket.

'An associate?' I asked. 'What's that?'

'It means they committed crimes together,' the police officer explained.

I sensed that Dad was getting impatient to go to the beach, now that the sun was shining, and I knew that Stinky would be really eager to get out of my pocket.

'Can we go now?' I asked the police officer.

She nodded and smiled.

'You'd make an excellent police officer one day, young man,' she said. 'You're very observant – unlike some other people I could mention.'

My dad and Ted Slim looked very sheepish indeed.

Chapter 7

Back at the holiday apartment my mum
was putting the final touches to our pirate
costumes for tonight's fancy-dress disco.
Lucy was tap-dancing, as usual. But when my
dad and I burst in, the sewing and the tapping
stopped at once.

'You'll never guess what happened at the
museum,' Dad said excitedly. 'There was a
crime. The police came!'

Lucy gasped and her eyes lit up. 'Did Ben
get arrested?'

'No,' said my dad, frowning. 'Of course not.'

She looked a bit disappointed.

'A man stole something,' Dad continued, 'and Ben here was a witness.'

As he told them the story, I sneaked off to my room and popped Stinky back into his cage. He must have been really tense after

spending so long in my pocket, because he
went straight to his wheel and ran for ages.

Later, I put the pad of paper next to his
cage and opened it to where I'd scribbled the
shopping list, so he could have a good look at it.
'Any clues?'

He glared at me.

'Give me a minute!' he said. 'If you had been hiding from a robber and, moreover, spent an extremely long time in the pocket of a very fidgety boy, you would need time to recover too.'

So I sat on the bed and tried to give Stinky some thinking time. But it was really hard to be patient when there was such an exciting mystery to solve.

'That man,' I whispered, 'Larry Skinner – he must think there's a clue in that note too.'

'Certainly,' said Stinky. 'Which means that we need to be quick, or else he'll find the diamonds before we do.'

'But it looks just like an ordinary shopping list to me,' I said.

Stinky shook his head.

'There's something rather odd about it,' he said. 'For instance, guavas – quite unusual fruit, don't you think? Especially all those years ago, when the note was written. And two Brussels sprouts.

Doesn't that strike you as strange?'

'Even one Brussels sprout,' I agreed, 'is one Brussels sprout too many.'

'No, Ben,' he said with a sigh. 'I mean, who would only buy a pair of sprouts? There is something most peculiar about the quantities.'

'But what does it all mean?'

'That's what I might be able to work out,' he snapped, 'if I had a bit of peace and quiet.'

So I left him alone – for a few hours, because we went to the beach.

When I came back, Stinky had some startling news for me.

Chapter 8

'I know where the diamonds are!' Stinky exclaimed.

'Where?'

'Under a tree!'

I frowned at him.

'I know you haven't spent much time outdoors, Stinky, but there are thousands of trees around. Millions probably.'

'The particular tree we are looking for, however, is in the shape of the letter *V*.'

Perhaps Stinky had lost his mind. Maybe all

that time in my pocket had made him crazy.

'It's in the shopping list,' he said. 'Have a look. What's the first item on there?'

'Three sausages,' I said.

'Three sausages. Exactly. And what's the third letter of "sausages"?'

I spelled it out, counting on my fingers.

'*U*,' I said.

'Correct. So, get your pen and circle the *U* on the list. Now, "four oranges" – what's the fourth letter of "oranges"?'

'*N?*'

'Exactly – circle it, and the fifth letter of "bread", and so on.'

When I'd finished, I read the message that I'd circled.

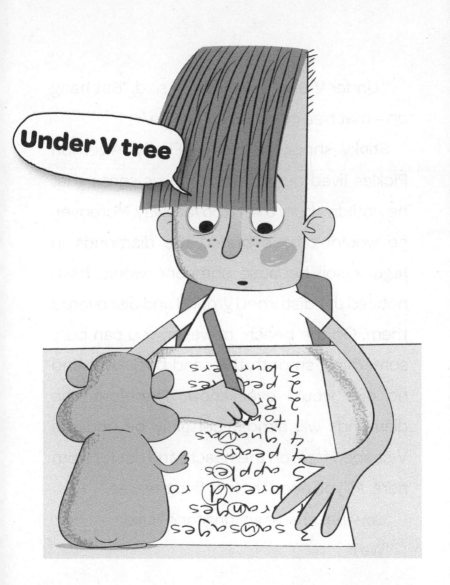

'"Under V tree" – brilliant!' I said. 'But hang on – that tree could be anywhere.'

Stinky shook his head. 'Firstly, Algernon Pickles lived nearby, so it makes sense that he wouldn't bury them too far away. Moreover, he wouldn't have buried the diamonds in regular soil because someone would have noticed the disturbed ground and discovered them. On the beach, however, you can bury something, smooth the sand back over and no one would ever know. Therefore, the diamonds will almost certainly be under a V-shaped tree, on the beach, and not far from here. All *you* need to do is find the tree.'

'So, what are we waiting for?' I said.

'We?'

'Let's go out, find the tree-that-looks-like-a-V and dig up the treasure!'

Stinky shook his head.

'I've had more than enough excitement for today, thank you. I'm going to have myself a well-earned nap. It's your turn to do some of the work.'

Then he waggled his bottom at me and disappeared into his little house.

So I went to see my mum, who was sprawled on the sofa, reading her book.

'Can I go back to the beach for a bit, Mum?'

She looked up at me, putting her finger on the page so she wouldn't lose her place.

'The beach?' she said, frowning. 'We've just been there, Ben.'

'Just for a short while. Please.'

She shook her head.

'We'll have to put on our costumes for the fancy-dress disco soon,' she said. 'And I know how long you take to get ready. You're slower than an elderly tortoise.'

Then she went back to her book. I could tell that she was at a really exciting bit, and that gave me an idea.

'If I get into my costume first,' I said, 'and promise to stay away from the water, can I pop to the beach for just a few minutes? There aren't any roads to cross.' Without looking up, she sighed, nodded and pointed to the costume on the table.

I got dressed in two minutes flat.

There were ragged
'pirate' trousers,
a stripy shirt,
an eyepatch,
a bandana, a
waistcoat and,
finally, a plastic
parrot to clip
onto my shoulder.

I looked in the
mirror and blushed.

I would feel
incredibly stupid
walking around like that, but I was desperate
to find the diamonds before that horrible man
got to them, and there was no time to lose.

I dashed to my room to pick up my bucket and spade.

Stinky wasn't asleep yet. He peered at me from inside his house.

'If it isn't Short John Silver,' he said with a chuckle.

'Please, Stinky, come and help me find the diamonds,' I pleaded. 'Three eyes are better than one,' I added, pointing to my eyepatch.

'I am not getting into your pocket again, if that's what you're thinking. Or into a bucket for that matter.'

'I've got a better idea,' I said. 'This parrot is hollow.' I tapped it to demonstrate. 'I can put you inside, and there's a little hole in its tummy you can see out of.'

He stared at me for a while, and then he sighed, came out of his house and said, 'OK.'

I grinned.

'I must be crazy,' he said.

Chapter 9

When you're pacing up and down the beach wearing a pirate costume, with a plastic parrot on your shoulder, everyone thinks they can laugh at you. I was searching for the tree when I walked past a man and a woman who were sitting on deck chairs.

'Don't make me walk the plank, me hearty!' the man said in a pirate voice, grinning.

'Looking for buried treasure, matey?' joked the woman.

'I am actually,' I said, which made them

both giggle. 'You don't know where there's a V-shaped tree around here, do you?' I asked, but they both shook their heads and laughed some more.

It was Stinky who spotted the tree, and straight away I ran down the beach towards it.

It's not so easy, running on soft sand with a parrot balanced on your shoulder. Plus Stinky was getting queasy.

'It's like your dad's driving all over again,' he panted. 'Being jiggled this way and that.'

So I walked the rest of the way.

As soon as we reached the tree, I got down on my hands and knees and started digging.

The plan (which Stinky had whispered into my ear as we were walking) was to dig a big circle around the tree, like I was making a deep moat. But it wasn't long before I realised that this would take me absolutely ages, especially as I only had a tiny plastic spade.

'Can't you help, Stinky? You're a great burrower. How about you dig in the sand for the treasure with me?'

'Certainly not,' he said. 'There might be crabs in there. Do you know what happens when crabs meet hamsters?'

'No.'

'Me neither, but I have no intention of finding out. They have *pincers*, you know. Not paws, or hands, but deadly weapons!'

So I kept on digging by myself.

Stinky was whispering encouragement in my ear, which helped a bit, but digging for treasure was really hard work. After half an hour I'd found three bottle tops and a crisp packet, but no diamonds at all. My pirate costume was all sweaty, my back was aching and I was exhausted.

'We should go back,' said Stinky. 'It's getting dark, your mum will be worried and you'll be in an extremely large amount of trouble if you're late. We can always come back tomorrow.'

'But what if Larry Skinner cracks the code and finds the diamonds before we come back? I feel like we're so close.'

I started digging faster and faster – sand was flying everywhere – but, after a few more minutes, I stopped, out of breath. My whole body ached, and Stinky was right – an angry Mum wasn't worth the risk, not for all the diamonds in the world.

'OK, Stinky,' I said. 'Let's –'

I didn't finish the sentence because I'd spotted some dark green material poking out of the sand beneath me.

I quickly dug around it. It was a small bag, no bigger than my hand.

I scooped my fingers underneath and pulled it out carefully.

It was tied at the top in a very tight triple knot, which I couldn't untie no matter how hard I tried.

'Let me help,' said Stinky, so I took him out of the parrot, put him onto my palm and held the knot in front of him. He nibbled away at it with his sharp teeth and, in no time, he'd gnawed it open.

'Now put me back immediately,' he said, 'before a seagull spots me and thinks I'm dinner.'

When I'd put him back inside the parrot, I looked around to make sure nobody was looking and then poured the contents of the bag into my hand.

Eight little pink diamonds, each of them glinting in the moonlight.

'Wow!' I said. 'Actual real-life treasure.'

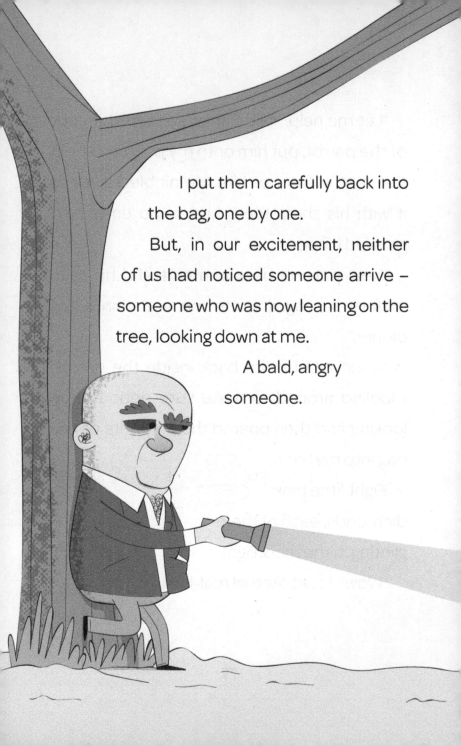

I put them carefully back into the bag, one by one.

But, in our excitement, neither of us had noticed someone arrive – someone who was now leaning on the tree, looking down at me.

A bald, angry someone.

Chapter 10

'**Y**ou've got something that belongs to me, kid,' Larry Skinner said in a slow, icy voice. 'Give me that bag.'

In one hand he had a garden spade. In the other he had a torch, which he shone into my eyes as I stood in the hole that I'd dug.

'Wait – you're the kid from the museum,' he said,

frowning and leaning forward. 'Who *are* you? Why are you dressed like a pirate? And how the devil did you know where to come to look for the diamonds.'

I was so frightened I could hardly breathe, let alone speak.

'The contents of that bag you are clutching in that shaky hand of yours,' he continued, 'are mine.'

I shook my head and this seemed to make him even angrier. His eyes bulged and his nostrils flared.

'I was personal friends with the gentleman who buried that bag,' he said. 'We worked together for a while. I opened doors for him. And when he went to prison, he told me that if anything happened to him, he'd leave a note with a code so I'd know exactly where the diamonds were hidden.

'And then he went and died – death by broccoli, the very worst way to go. The problem for me was, I couldn't get hold of that note. Until now. And I've waited far too long to let a snotty little kid in a pirate costume get in the way. So –' he glared at me and cracked his knuckles – 'hand me that bag you've so kindly saved me the trouble of digging up. Then I can go home. And you won't get hurt.'

I was still too scared to say anything. Instead it was my hamster who spoke.

'Those diamonds simply do not belong to you, Skinner,' he said.

Larry Skinner's eyes almost popped out of his head. He shone his torch at me, and then at the parrot on my shoulder.

'Who said that?'

'Me,' said Stinky. 'The parrot.'

'That's a plastic bird!' Skinner jabbered. 'How can it talk? And how does it know my name?' He shook his head. 'I'm imagining things,' he muttered to himself.

'The only thing that you're imagining,' said Stinky, 'is that you might get away with this.'

Larry Skinner angrily jabbed his spade towards me.

'Do you want me to come down there, wring that parrot's birdy neck and whack you on your noggin? Because I'll do it. I'm not a violent man – not usually – but this is your very last chance, you little snake. Give. Me. That. Bag.'

'Any ideas, Stinky?' I whispered to the parrot, my heart thumping.

'None at all,' he said sadly. 'I think you'd better give him the diamonds.'

So I climbed shakily out of the hole. Larry Skinner edged over to me.

'No funny business, kid,' he said. 'I've got a spade, and I'm not afraid to use it.'

Just as I was about to hand him the bag though, I heard something behind me: quick footsteps and heavy breathing.

I looked over my shoulder.

There, in pirate costumes, looking as ridiculous as I did, were my family.

I'd never been so pleased to see them.

Chapter 11

My mum looked so angry she might explode. At first I thought she must be mad at me for being late, and she probably was, but it was Larry Skinner she was glaring at.

'You just threatened my son,' she said.

She'd painted a scar on her face and had a hook instead of a right hand. Even on good days, she was terrifying when she was angry. But right now she was Larry Skinner's worst nightmare.

'What do you have to say for yourself?'

she went on, prodding her hook at him. 'Threatening a nine-year-old boy. You should be absolutely ashamed.'

My dad pulled out his cutlass from its scabbard and pointed it at Skinner. (It was a plastic cutlass, but it *looked* real.)

Larry Skinner was petrified.

'A whole pirate family,' he muttered, looking around. 'A talking plastic parrot. I must be in a very bad dream. Wake up!' he said to himself.

It was then that he started pinching himself.

'Owww!' he yelped. 'But they're still here!
Must do it harder. Wake up! Owwwww!'

This went on for a while, until he finally
stopped pinching himself, took one last look at

each of us, dropped
his spade and torch
and ran off. He was
really fast for an old
man, although he
did lose his balance
a couple of times
and landed face
first in the sand.

We watched him run away.

'What did he mean, a talking parrot?' asked Lucy.

I shrugged.

'You're late, Benjamin Jinks,' Mum said, frowning at me now.

This time I didn't shrug. I knew I was in trouble, and my mum isn't such a big fan of shrugging at the best of times.

'We were worried,' she said. 'We didn't know where you were. Luckily a couple heading home from the beach pointed us in your direction.'

'Sorry, Mum,' I said. 'I was going to come back. But then I found some treasure. And that man wanted to take it off me.'

'Treasure?' said Dad, raising his eyebrows.

I gave him the little green bag and he peered inside.

'Diamonds!' he said, picking one out and studying it in the moonlight. 'Nice ones too.'

'Diamonds?' Lucy squealed. 'I've always wanted a real one! Can we keep them?'

Mum shook her head.

'There are many more important things in life than diamonds, Lucy,' she said. 'Besides, they're not ours. We're going to take them to the police station, right away.'

We marched off together, my mum leading the way.

The police officer on duty at the station was very surprised to see a family dressed as pirates, and even more surprised when my dad carefully opened the bag and poured the diamonds onto the counter in front of him.

'My son here dug them up on the beach,' he said proudly.

The police officer was dumbstruck for a bit, but eventually he grinned and said, 'It certainly makes a very pleasant change, pirates *returning* treasure, rather than stealing it.' Then he shook his head and added, 'It never fails to surprise me, this job.'

Chapter 12

Everyone enjoyed the fancy-dress disco. Well, everyone apart from Stinky.

Lucy had a great time because she was able to dance for hours.

My dad was over the moon because our family won the fancy-dress competition.

My mum was happy too, because the prize was a huge box of chocolates She told us she preferred chocolates to diamonds, any day of the week.

I was feeling great because we'd solved

another mystery. The jeweller had even given us a cash reward. Also, I was quite relieved that I hadn't been hit with a spade.

Only Stinky was grumpy, and I could understand why – after the police station, we'd gone straight to the disco, and he'd had to stay inside the parrot the whole time. I think he was muttering complaints about the music into my ear most of the night, but luckily it was hard to hear him with all the noise. He wasn't too happy to be jiggled around by my dance moves either.

He cheered up the next day though.

I put five perfect carrots in his cage for breakfast, and then let him nap and eat for most of the day while we went to the beach.

When I got back to my room, I was holding a sheet of newspaper.

'About time,' he said. 'My cage needs a thorough clean from top to bottom.'

'I'm not cleaning your bottom.'

'Not *my* bottom,' he snapped. 'The bottom of my cage.'

'Oh,' I said.

So I cleaned his cage, but the fresh sheet of newspaper that I put down inside it was a very special one. The headline said:

PIRATE BOY UNCOVERS MISSING DIAMONDS

Stinky grinned as he read it.

There was no mention of a hamster, of course. But that's just how Stinky likes it.

THE END

Have you read all the
Stinky and Jinks adventures?

Piccadilly
PRESS

Dave Lowe grew up in Dudley in the West Midlands, and now lives in Brisbane, Australia, with his wife and two daughters. He spends his days writing books, drinking lots of tea, and treading on Lego that his daughters have left lying around. Dave's Stinky and Jinks books follow the adventures of a nine-year-old boy called Ben, and Stinky, Ben's genius pet hamster. (When Dave was younger, he had a pet hamster too. Unlike Stinky, however, Dave's hamster didn't often help him with his homework.) Find Dave online at @daveloweauthor or www.davelowebooks.com

Born in York in the late 1970s, **The Boy Fitz Hammond** now lives in Edinburgh with his wife and their two sons. A freelance illustrator for well over a decade, he loves to draw in a variety of styles, allowing him to work on a range of projects across all media. Find him online at www.nbillustration.co.uk/the-boy-fitz-hammond or on Twitter @tbfhDotCom

Thank you for choosing a Piccadilly Press book.

If you would like to know more about our authors, our books or if you'd just like to know what we're up to, you can find us online.

www.piccadillypress.co.uk

You can also find us on:

We hope to see you soon!